VIENNA WOLFE

(THE IMPERIAL SEASON 3.5)

DE WOLFE PACK
THE SERIES

MARY LANCASTER

DE WOLFE PACK: THE SERIES

By Alexa Aston
Rise of de Wolfe

By Amanda Mariel
Love's Legacy

By Anna Markland
Hungry Like de Wolfe

By Autumn Sands
Reflection of Love

By Barbara Devlin
Lone Wolfe: Heirs of Titus De Wolfe Book 1
The Big Bad De Wolfe: Heirs of Titus De Wolfe Book 2
Tall, Dark & De Wolfe: Heirs of Titus De Wolfe Book 3

By Cathy MacRae
The Saint

By Christy English
Dragon Fire

By Hildie McQueen
The Duke's Fiery Bride

By Kathryn Le Veque
River's End

By Lana Williams
Trusting the Wolfe

By Laura Landon
A Voice on the Wind

By Leigh Lee
Of Dreams and Desire

By Mairi Norris
Brabanter's Rose

By Marlee Meyers
The Fall of the Black Wolf

By Mary Lancaster
Vienna Wolfe

By Meara Platt
Nobody's Angel
Bhrodi's Angel
Kiss an Angel

By Mia Pride
The Lone Wolf's Lass

By Ruth Kaufman
My Enemy, My Love

By Sarah Hegger
Bad Wolfe on the Rise

By Scarlett Cole
Together Again

By Victoria Vane
Breton Wolfe Book 1
Ivar the Red Book 2
The Bastard of Brittany Book 3

By Violetta Rand
Never Cry de Wolfe

TABLE OF CONTENTS

CHAPTER ONE

WITHOUT DOUBT, ELISE caused the accident by daydreaming. Lost in her own thoughts of a certain nobleman known as the English Wolf, she paid no attention to her surroundings until a horse and laden cart swerved to avoid her. Unfortunately, the carter drove straight into the path of a magnificent, white stallion which reared up in fury, all plunging hooves and tossing head as it screamed in outrage.

Even then, Elise could have saved herself by simply moving out of the way. But her gaze was riveted to the beautiful, white horse and its dark, powerful rider who held on with hands and knees of apparent iron. She found herself too stunned to move. Surely, the English Wolf himself.

The rider clearly had control. The stallion's dangerous hooves would have come back to earth without further incident, if only its behavior hadn't, in turn, frightened the cart horse, which bolted onward, dragging the cart right into the way of the flying hooves.

It was only one kick, but it couldn't have been better placed for maximum carnage. One of the traces broke and the laden cart tipped up. Only then, as barrels plunged directly at her, did Elise stumble backward to save herself.

However, the street was narrow and her reaction was unforgivably slow. A glancing blow against her shoulder sent her sprawling to the ground amidst a hail of her own heavy parcels. Something struck her ankle, causing it to twist with agonizing pain.

Amidst the cries of horror and anger, a deep, male voice issued sharp commands in English and then repeated them in German. Through the haze of her pain and humiliation, Elise was aware that the noise had quieted, that the horses were calm and the carter's boy and several passers-by by were moving the fallen barrels. The white stallion stood riderless but still, its reins held close by a slim gentleman at its head. Not its rider. She was sure she'd recognized quite a different gentleman in the saddle. Unless her imagination had been playing tricks.

A kindly Viennese woman in a flowered bonnet

bent over Elise, asking her if she was hurt, offering to help her rise.

"Thank you, I'm fine," Elise managed. The pain in her ankle seemed to be fading until she moved and had to bite her lip to stop from yelping.

"You're not fine at all," said an irritated male voice on her other side. It was the same voice that had been issuing commands to bring order into the chaos she'd caused.

Elise turned her head quickly and gazed into the harshly handsome face of Colonel Francis Wolfe, Earl of Warenton, the English Wolf himself.

She'd been right. He had, indeed, been the rider of the white stallion—which was certainly ironic if not downright humiliating, considering the silly stuff of her daydreams when she'd walked into the cart.

"Where do you hurt?" Beneath straight, black brows, his dark eyes scanned the length of her person, perhaps for signs of blood, until they came to rest on her face.

She'd never been close enough to actually look into his eyes before. From a distance, they'd seemed to match the rest of him—commanding, perceptive, handsome, down-to-earth and quite impersonal, with just a hint of aristocratic haughtiness.

Well, he was, indeed, of a noble English family, and the commander of a crack regiment of dragoons which had distinguished itself many times in the fight against Napoleon Bonaparte. In fact, it was the French who'd first called him *Le Loup Anglais*. The recent, unexpected death of his older brother had made him Earl of Warenton, but even in the plain black coat he wore just now, he still looked every inch the soldier.

She'd no real idea why he, of all people, the man her employer's niece was pursuing for matrimonial purposes, should have become the subject of her foolish daydreams. Except that he was tall and handsome and capable, and immeasurably above most of the young, silly men who crossed her path. It was undeniably shocking to find herself this close to him as he crouched over her. And those eyes weren't impersonal at all. Beneath the impassive veil that was all the world saw, they seethed and boiled, though with what, she couldn't tell. She only hoped it wasn't anger.

"Is your horse hurt?" she blurted.

A quick frown twitched down his brow. "Of course not. But I think you are."

"No, no, I'm—" She broke off, breath hissing between her teeth as she again tried to rise.

At the same time, a hired green Imperial carriage rumbled by, narrowly missing Elise and Lord Warenton as it scraped by the damaged cart. Lord Warenton uttered something impatient under his breath, then simply swept her up in his arms and strode along the road.

Elise opened her mouth to protest at such high-handed treatment, but no words came out. She might have been a baby for all the effort he seemed to exert. And besides, the hard strength of his arms and the chest against which she lay was curiously intimidating. Without warning, he swerved right into a doorway a foot or so back from its neighbors and deposited Elise on the step with surprising gentleness.

Again he crouched beside her. "It's your ankle, isn't it?" And with no further warning, he shoved aside her skirt, exposing her ankle, and began to unlace her shoe.

"Sir!" she cried, outraged.

He cast her an even more impatient look while easing off her shoe with surprising gentleness. "Calm yourself, madam. Am I likely to assault you quite so publicly? I assure you, I have no designs upon your virtue."

"I never supposed you had," she replied honestly. "But neither am I used to being so handled!"

"Are you used to falling down in the street and being struck by rampaging barrels?" he inquired with more than a hint of sarcasm.

"No, that is new," she allowed. "Though I used to walk into walls and doors as a child."

His fingers encircled her ankle, causing her breath to catch. Her whole body flushed with embarrassment. Warenton gently yet firmly probed her ankle and the surrounding area.

He glanced up. "You walked into doors? Are you short-sighted?"

"No, just easily distracted," she admitted.

The ghost of a smile crossed his rather hard face and vanished so quickly that she wondered if she'd been mistaken.

"Thank you for your care," she said on a rush. "And I'm so sorry for startling your horse. I'm sure my ankle is quite recovered now. I really must get back."

Again, he glanced up from her ankle. With shock, she realized that her stockinged foot now rested on his muscular thigh.

"Back where?" he asked.

Just as she'd thought, he had no idea who she was.

"To my employer," she said calmly.

His gaze flickered over the strewn parcels as he untied and unraveled his neck cloth. "I'm sure your employer can wait five more minutes to receive you and your somewhat crushed parcels."

"Oh dear," Elise sighed, gazing at them in dismay. A stray dog was already tearing its way in to the lamb until some children shooed it away and began to gather up her parcels for her. The paints and brushes had clearly been run over. She would have to go out again.

She brought her slightly baffled attention back to the earl, who was quickly and efficiently binding his cravat around her ankle. Now that the pain was easing, she felt every touch, every brush of his skin on hers like a flame. The heat rushed through her body to her face.

"You're very kind, sir," she managed.

"Not in the slightest," he said impatiently. "It was my horse that caused the problem. He's a fierce war horse, but too skittish in the city. I shouldn't ride him here."

She blinked. "Was that an apology?"

Tearing a split in the ends of his makeshift bandage, he neatly tied it off before glancing up from his handiwork. "You sound surprised."

"I thought you never apologized."

It was certainly his reputation, according to Miss Sylvia, her employer's niece. But at her words, Elise was sure a veil dropped back over his eyes. For some reason, she thought he was disappointed.

"What is your name?" he asked.

"Elise de Sancerre."

She hadn't expected him to recognize the name and he clearly didn't. "Well, Mademoiselle, the bandage will give your ankle some support and protection. Fortunately, it does not appear to be broken. I suspect it's badly bruised, though, so it will be sore for several days. Allow me to summon you a cab."

"Oh no, please, I have not far to go." And she had no money to pay a hired carriage. Miss Renleigh would be outraged. On top of furious at the damage done to her parcels.

"Then I shall take you myself."

She stared, tensing as he slipped the shoe back on her foot and swiftly re-tied the laces. For the first time since her boots had finally disintegrated last winter, she thanked God she had only these shoes to wear on her feet. A boot would never have fitted over the bandage and would have hurt, besides.

Carefully, he lowered her foot to the bottom step and stood, clasping her fingers to draw her to her feet. Her hand jumped in his. Ridiculously, it seemed a more intimate touch than that on her ankle. Perhaps it was the fault of his overwhelming presence. Now that she stood beside him, he seemed immensely tall.

With his free hand, he flicked a coin to the two children guarding her ragged parcels. They grinned with delight, picking them up and preparing, clearly, to follow.

Warenton swung back to Elise, scowling down at her. "Don't you have gloves? Your hand is freezing."

And rough with the winter cold and careless needlework. She swallowed her shame. "I left them at home," she lied.

Unexpectedly, another smile flickered across his face. "You really *are* easily distracted, aren't you? What is it you think about while you freeze yourself to death and leap in front of wild horses?"

"A better world," she said ruefully.

His lips curved into a lopsided smile. "And I'm told young ladies are incapable of deep thought."

"I'm six and twenty, so not so young. Besides," she

added in the interests of honesty, "I only meant *my* world, which is a very narrow definition."

"Is it? Vienna during the Peace Congress is surely a broader world than most of us are used to."

"Vienna, yes," she allowed. "But I regret to inform you that the great rulers of Europe neglect to consult me."

She often threw away remarks like that. Usually no one listened and, if by some chance people heard, they never saw the humor.

"Fools," the earl said gravely, although his eyes danced beguilingly enough to deprive her of breath all over again.

In self-preservation, she dropped her gaze and discovered her hand still lost in his. Despite the pleasurable warmth, she began to snatch it back. Warenton held on, merely placing it in the crook of his arm instead. From instinct, she stepped forward when he did, wincing slightly as she took her weight on her sore foot.

"Lean on me," he ordered.

"Thank you," she muttered.

"You are French," he observed.

"Yes. You are doubly kind to help the enemy."

"That's not my reputation, either. Is that how you think of me?"

Le Loup Anglais. The English Wolf... She blinked. "As kind? Of course!"

"As the enemy," he said wryly.

Elise, who had always known she was foolish to think of him at all, said only, "You are a soldier, are you not? You have been fighting the French for a long time."

"I remember. You're not giving much away, are you?"

"It's my nature. If you have a question, ask me." Never had it entered her head that he would speak to her at all, unless it was *Will you tell Miss Renleigh I am here* or *Pass the milk*. He had been in her company several times before this. The realization that he finally saw her both thrilled and terrified her.

She kept her attention on the ground, barely feeling the discomfort of her injured ankle. *Step, limp, step, limp. Don't lean on him...* And yet, she felt his gaze burning into the side of her face.

"Why did you look at me like that?"

Her eyes flew up to his. Whatever she had expected, it was not that. "Like what? When?"

He gave an impatient shrug. "When you first looked round at me. As if I'd saved you rather than injured you."

Heat surged into her cheeks and she tore her gaze free. "You're mistaken, sir. I accuse you of neither. Though I am grateful for your assistance."

He waved that aside if her words annoyed him. Nervously, she saw that they were approaching the turning into Fahrengasse. If either of the Renleigh ladies were to see her now, or even *hear* about her walking arm in arm with Lord Warenton, her life would not be worth living.

He muttered, "I don't ask for your gratitude. I don't wish it."

"Well, I cannot help that you have it," she said lightly. "However, if you would assist me in one more thing…?"

"Of course," he said at once, although she was sure that disappointment flickered, once more, in his gaze. Clearly, he thought she would ask him for money or favors of some kind. After all, she must look as if she needed them. And since he'd inherited his brother's earldom, he must have been pursued relentlessly by fortune hunters and other greedy women.

"Leave me here," she said quietly, coming to a halt. "I find I can walk quite easily and the children will carry my shopping for me."

Only by the faintest twitch of his brow did he reveal his surprise.

With difficulty, she held his gaze. "Neither my reputation nor my post would survive my arriving on your arm."

"Is my own reputation so dire?" he asked with a disarming hint of ruefulness.

In truth, there were rumors of a Spanish contessa, several actresses and a minor member of the Bonaparte family, but those ladies were not Elise's problem. "It is *my* position which is delicate," she admitted.

He searched her face with alarmingly perceptive eyes. "Very well. Only, tell me where I may inquire about your recovery."

She shook her head.

"But I will see you again," he said with certainty.

Her smile was born of sadness as well as self-deprecating amusement. "No, you won't see me again."

Something in her intonation must have bothered him, for a quick frown tugged down his brow.

She drew her hand free of his arm and stepped

back, holding it out to him instead. "Goodbye, sir."

"*Au revoir*," he returned, though he took her hand and bowed over it punctiliously.

She slipped free, tearing her gaze from his, and limped on. For a moment, she was afraid he would simply stand and watch her to see where she went, but he must have realized how singular that would appear to everyone in the street, including his friend who still held the restive stallion. As it was, she would be lucky if this story didn't reach the gossip mongers.

CHAPTER TWO

HAVING RETRIEVED AND stabled his horse, which was none the worse for its adventure, Lord Warenton returned to his sister's apartment near St. Stephen's Cathedral. He discovered Lady Caroline in her sitting room with her maid, trying to decide between two brocade trims which looked exactly the same to him.

"This is infuriating," Caroline exclaimed. "They are both so pretty, it will make me cry if I can't make up my mind. Francis, which should I wear to the Renleighs' masquerade?"

"The one on the left," Warenton said randomly.

"You are quite right," Caroline agreed with obvious relief. "Even if you didn't actually look at them. This one, Cardew. It is clearly superior."

"Clearly," Warenton murmured.

"What will you wear, Francis?" Caroline asked as the maid hurried from the room.

"My regimentals," Warenton said at once. "Masquerading as a soldier."

Caroline eyed him sideways. "You don't *need* to leave the army, you know. There are other people who can run the estates perfectly well without you."

"It isn't the same, though, and it isn't right," he said, throwing himself into the vacant chair near her. "Besides, most of us will be on half-pay soon anyway. Not much need of soldiers in peace time. Don't pay any attention to my whining. It's not that I mind stepping into George's shoes. I just wish he was still wearing them."

Caroline swallowed and reached for her handkerchief. "So do I," she snuffled into it, then lowered it and smiled at him encouragingly. "But in truth, Francis, you never whined. I just know how much you always loved the army. It was never meant to be this way, was it? You were meant to be a general one day."

He shrugged. "I'd be a rotten general. I may well prove to be a rotten earl, too, but at least no one will tell me what to do." He frowned suddenly. "Talking of being told what to do, *must* I go to this damned ball? I hate masquerades."

"Well, of course you must go! I already told Miss

Renleigh and Sylvia that you would be there. You're practically the guest of honor."

"In a mask," he said disparagingly. "What's the point of that?"

"You don't need to wear it. It's just a bit of fun. And most fashionable here in Vienna. Everyone who is anyone holds masked balls. Besides, it could be romantic. You could propose to Sylvia before the unmasking."

He cast her a sardonic glance. "What if I propose to the wrong lady by mistake? Besides, you have quite the wrong idea about Sylvia if you imagine she is remotely romantic. Like any well-bred young woman, she is marrying the position not the person."

Caroline, halfway to the door, paused to glance back at him curiously. No one had ever accused her of a lack of perception. "That sounds like a criticism. I thought this was what you wanted? A well-bred lady to run your households and bear you heirs."

"It didn't work for George, did it?" Warenton retorted.

"Well, I always felt he could have tried harder," Caroline said candidly. "Too many opera dancers and not enough time at home with his wife."

"He should have married a more agreeable lady. Honoria would drive a saint into the arms of opera dancers. Plural."

"Francis!" she exclaimed, in shocked tones that didn't fool Warenton for a moment.

"You brought the subject up."

Caroline waved that aside. Instead of leaving, she came back into the room and sat down beside him. "You do find Sylvia agreeable, do you not? You did say you liked her best of all the suitable candidates I suggested."

Warenton shifted restlessly. For some reason, the big, dark eyes of the pretty French girl swam back into his wayward mind. A sweet face with most kissable lips beneath a tired old bonnet. Within her oft-mended gown and cloak, her figure had been trim and desirable, even if she had felt so light and frail and curiously vulnerable in his arms. A mysterious lady of undoubted attractions.

But more than that, she was *different*. Unexpected. She had depths, passions. The way she had looked at him when he'd first crouched down beside her—a strange mixture of intense pleasure, gratitude and fear that he was at a loss to account for. Especially since she'd been so keen to dismiss him. Even though—or perhaps because—she knew exactly who he was.

"Maybe agreeable isn't enough," he said aloud. "Shouldn't there be more to leg-shackling yourself for life to someone?"

"If she's agreeable now, there *will* be more," Caroline promised him. "As there is for Vernon and me."

"Vernon was always a good chap. And good company… *Is* Sylvia agreeable?"

"You said she was."

"So I did," he recalled, getting to his feet. "But the truth is, I wouldn't miss her if I never saw her again." In fact, if she ran off with a gypsy, he'd probably be relieved.

Still, he had to marry someone, now that he was earl. And, moreover, an earl who traced his ancestry back to the Conquest and his title back to the thirteenth century needed to marry an equally well-bred woman. He owed that to his family. Caroline was right. Sylvia was also a scion of an ancient, noble lineage. She would run his houses efficiently and make an excellent countess. She knew all that was expected of her. She was pretty enough, too, and accomplished. At the age of one and twenty, she had already turned down two eligible suitors, which, oddly enough, was what had endeared her to Warenton in the first place. That she was picky.

Only now did it occur to him, somewhat cynically, that she'd turned down an untitled gentleman and a mere baronet. She might have come to Vienna in search of a prince—God knew they were practically ten a penny here right now—but she'd make do with an earl.

He was at the door before, from sudden impulse, he turned back again. "Do you know any of the French émigrés here, Caro?"

"You think you might prefer old but grateful aristocracy?" Caroline said irreverently. "You're too late for the gratitude. They'll all go back to France and be rich again."

"A few might, but I doubt many can bank on it."

"Why are you interested?"

"No reason." Warenton murmured and went out. He wanted to find out who and where—and how—Elise de Sancerre was, but he had no intention of revealing his reasons to his sister. For one thing, he wasn't sure what they were.

〉〉〉〉〈〈〈〈

ON THE DAY following her accident, the day of the Renleighs' masquerade, Elise was run ragged with a million trivial tasks. By the time the ladies were actually dressing for the event, her ankle ached almost as much as it had when she'd first returned to the tall, thin house in the Fahrengasse, laden with her torn and tatty parcels.

She hadn't explained to Miss Renleigh all that had happened, saying only that she'd fallen in the street on the way home and hurt her ankle.

Miss Renleigh had glared at her. "What deplorable timing, Mamzelle!" She always called Elise *Mamzelle* so that sometimes it seemed to be her actual name. "You knew I was counting on you. Tomorrow is vitally important to us."

"I'm sure I'll be able to cope, Miss Renleigh," she said optimistically.

Miss Renleigh sniffed. "The cost of the ruined meat and the paints will be kept from your salary. Might teach you to be more careful."

Elise, who'd expected nothing else, didn't even sigh. Once, she'd naively imagined saving enough money to leave Miss Renleigh's employ and becoming a governess instead. Or opening a hat shop. Or running away on a pirate ship. One was as likely as another.

Miss Renleigh preferred the way Elise dressed her hair to her maid's efforts, but for the ball, nothing pleased her and she ended by hitting Elise with the hairbrush. "Bring me the ruby tiara instead," she snapped. "Perhaps we can still disguise your mess!"

"Miss Sylvia has the tiara tonight," Elise reminded her, rubbing the sore ear where the brush had struck her.

Miss Renleigh scowled. "It's a masquerade. Everyone will know who she is if she wears the tiara, however many masks she has on!"

"They will know who you are, too," Elise pointed out.

"Who cares? I'm an old woman. My niece is about to make a brilliant marriage. She has to play the game. I simply watch. Go and get the tiara from her and bring it to me."

Elise limped out of Miss Renleigh's bedchamber and made her way along the passage to Miss Sylvia's.

Sylvia looked beautiful, like a perfect, porcelain

doll. Tall, regal and angelically fair, she wore a pure white, muslin gown trimmed with blue, exactly the same shade as her clear, cool eyes. Her maid was just lowering the tiara on to her blonde head when Elise limped in.

"Miss Renleigh says you should not wear the tiara tonight, that it will reveal your identity too early. She wants me to bring it back to her."

A flash of smugness on the maid's face told Elise that Sylvia had already received and ignored this advice. Sylvia knocked the maid's hand aside with enough force to dislodge the tiara which tumbled to the floor.

"Take it," Sylvia uttered with deep discontent. "It's an ugly thing anyway. I thought it might make me look regal." She shrugged impatiently, while Elise bent and picked the heavy tiara off the floor. "But maybe it's for the best. I shall be regal *after* I'm married. Or at least engaged."

Elise's heart seemed to twist. At first, she'd thought it was her dislike of Sylvia that caused her ill-natured wish for the pursued earl not to marry her. But in truth, there had always been something more to him, more than the cold, shallow Sylvia deserved. At least in

Elise's eyes. And yet, the man had never looked at Elise or spoken to her until yesterday's accident.

Still, unnoticed, she had observed him well over the last few weeks. A hint of self-deprecating humor had lurked behind his words and his occasional sardonic smile at those of others. That had intrigued her, together with the knowledge that Colonel Wolfe was a greatly honored soldier, a hero amongst Wellington's army of heroes. A large, quiet man with a commanding presence, never afraid to speak his mind, although he never seemed to rush to impose his views either. A clever man, who thought quickly, saw all sides, assessed and made judgments. An unexpectedly kind man, as she'd discovered yesterday morning. With rather beautiful, brown eyes steeped in tragedy beneath the surface he showed the world. A strong and handsome man whose hands had already touched her more intimately than those of any other… Sensitive—

"What are you waiting for, Mademoiselle?" Sylvia snapped, breaking into her reverie like a brutal discord in a tranquil piece of music.

"Nothing," Elise murmured, hastily limping away with the tiara.

"What the devil took you so long?" Miss Renleigh

demanded as she reentered the bedchamber.

"Sorry, Miss Renleigh," Elise said automatically. She set the dazzling tiara amongst the iron grey hair, but before she could pin it in place, Miss Renleigh snatched it from her head with irritation.

"It's all wrong. And will look stupid with a mask." Contemptuously, she threw the tiara several feet across the room to the bed. "I shall have to make do like this. After all, my niece is the belle of the ball." In the mirror, she caught Elise's gaze and frowned. "I shall want you close by my side, Mamzelle."

Elise's heart sank. She'd hoped for the night to herself, to rest her aching ankle and read a novel until she fell asleep to the sounds of the gaiety below. "Of course, Miss Renleigh. Only…why?"

Miss Renleigh glared. "For whatever reason I wish! To carry messages to my niece, to the servants or anyone else I choose. To carry out my wishes as is your function as my companion! Go and change into your other gown."

Her other gown was equally old, darned and unfashionable, though it had once had pretensions of being evening wear.

"Should I wear a mask as well?" she asked, with the

faint hope of at least having some fun out of the evening.

But Miss Renleigh flared her nostrils in disapproval. "Of course not. You're not a *guest*."

Elise left once more and trailed along the passage to the stairs, where she encountered Lord Renleigh, a fashionable young gentleman of two and twenty, who had just leapt down them three at a time. Arriving at the bottom, he immediately grabbed Elise and waltzed her wildly around the passage, to the further detriment of her poor ankle, until she managed to yank herself free.

"What has put you into such high spirits?" she demanded.

"Everything," his lordship enthused. "But mostly, the word is that Warenton's going to pop the question to my sister tonight, which means he'll be good for a tap."

Elise blinked. "You really mean to borrow money from him as soon as he and Miss Sylvia are engaged?"

"Why not? He'll expect it," Renleigh said cheerfully.

"Best not disappoint him then," Elise said with sarcasm.

"Exactly," Renleigh agreed and went on his way with a grin.

By far the most congenial of the Renleigh family, the young baron was, Elise had to concede, nevertheless equally grasping, self-centered and lazy. Although she suspected he might be in for a shock. Somehow, she couldn't quite see Lord Warenton happily handing out large wads of cash to fund Renleigh's predilections for gambling and expensive actresses.

⟫⟫⟫⟪⟪⟪

FROM HER HARD seat in the shadow of the ballroom stairs, Elise saw the Earl of Warenton arrive, together with his sister and her husband. Lady Caroline and Mr. Vernon were both easily recognizable, despite their masks. Lord Warenton didn't even trouble to wear his, although it dangled from his fingers carelessly as he bowed over Miss Renleigh's hand.

Prepared as she was, Elise couldn't prevent the sudden tumbling sensation in her heart.

In truth, he had always had something of that effect on her. She could never understand why when he only ever looked through her. Even when he'd knelt before her, her foot on his thigh and her ankle between his sure fingers, looking directly into her face, he'd had no idea that they'd ever met before. Because she, as a mere companion, was so far beneath him? Or because he was too dazzled by Sylvia?

Before yesterday, it had hardly mattered. Even now that she'd spoken to him, gained his attention for half an hour and made him smile, it shouldn't matter. Yet as he strolled into the ballroom, idly twirling his mask by its strings around one finger, her heart galloped without her permission. She couldn't drag her gaze away.

Always a distinguished man, in his red and gold-braided regimental coat and black pantaloons, he looked magnificent—large, broad-shouldered and powerful. And yet, he moved with easy elegance, unusual in so big a man.

He made some sardonic remark to Mr. Vernon, who laughed with clear amusement. A flicker of response lit the earl's face before he strolled away on his own, out of Elise's view. Searching, no doubt, for Sylvia.

Reluctantly, Elise returned her wayward gaze to Miss Renleigh who was, in fact, glaring at her. Elise flushed as she jumped to her feet and hurried the few yards to the old lady's side. Clearly Miss Renleigh had been trying to summon her for several moments and she must surely have seen the direction of Elise's attention.

"Find my niece," Miss Renleigh snapped. "Tell her Lord Warenton is here and not masked. And Mamzelle?"

"Yes, Miss Renleigh?"

"Do so discreetly."

"Of course."

In accordance with the long established rules of her presence at such events, she didn't plunge into the midst of the throng, but slipped around the edges. At such moments, she felt like a ghost, unseen and unreal, almost as if her whole person were slipping away into a mere phantom of herself.

If he saw her now, would he recognize her as the woman he'd helped yesterday? Or like everyone else, like every other occasion where they'd been in the same room, would he not see her at all?

Sylvia was dancing with the Russian Tsar, a notable distinction. They made a very handsome couple, each angelically tall and fair, and each wearing a charming, social smile. Although conversation appeared to be stilted. Well, Sylvia's French was appalling. Despite being here for several weeks where the common language among the international community was French, hers had never progressed beyond the very basic of the uninterested schoolgirl.

Elise waited patiently against the wall for the dance to end. She entertained herself by predicting where Sylvia would be when the music stopped and positioning herself accordingly. Pleased with her accuracy, she intercepted her quarry within a second of her leaving the dance floor, touched her arm to draw her attention and murmured Miss Renleigh's message. Sylvia bent her ear down to hear it, but otherwise didn't acknowledge Elise's presence.

Elise judged she now had a couple of minutes to herself before Miss Renleigh could accuse her of loitering, so she used it to wander around admiring the distinguished and beautiful among the guests. Prince Metternich himself, president of the Peace Congress, was present, urbane and affable and, no doubt, still working in his own peculiar way. The British delegation was also well represented, led by Lord and Lady Castlereagh, always recognizable for their eccentric dress, masked or not. Even Prince de Talleyrand, the

French representative, limped past her, in conversation with the Austrian von Gentz. To her surprise, his glance fell upon her as she passed and he inclined his head with civility. A moment later, she spotted his niece, the beautiful Dorothée, on the other side of the room, the center of a lively court of admirers.

Elise could tell herself she was interested in all of these people, in being near those who were making the historic peace of Europe. And on some level, she was. But in truth, she was really searching for the Earl of Warenton. Not to speak to him. Not even to bring herself to his notice, because she couldn't bear him to look through her as before. Or, worse, look down upon her in this company of the powerful and well-bred.

She still hadn't seen him by the time she came to the small antechamber. Ornamented with a large pot plant, a full length looking glass, a low, occasional table and a sofa, it had been designed for those seeking a brief respite from the hubbub of the main ballroom. Or for statesmen to have the discreet conversations that influenced the policy of the Congress. For this reason, Elise glanced quite warily inside. A sheaf of notepaper, two pens and an ink bottle had been thoughtfully provided on a side table, beside a decanter and four glasses.

However, the room was empty. She was about to carry on her circuit of the ballroom towards the card room—where she suspected the earl would be seen with his military friends—when an abandoned black mask caught her attention. On impulse, she slipped into the room and was immediately struck by the difference in noise. It really did give the impression of privacy and quiet.

Feeling guilty, Elise lowered herself onto the sofa and sighed with relief. One of the hardest things about being a companion was that one was never alone. Even at night, when she fell into bed, she could be summoned at any time because Miss Renleigh couldn't sleep or didn't feel well or just wanted to shout at someone. She could allow herself these two minutes...

However, only seconds later, she jumped up again, reaching for the abandoned mask on the table. By its size, it was a man's mask, although, made of plain black silk, it could have been worn by either sex.

Limping to the mirror, Elise held the mask over her eyes and laughed out loud at her reflection. Since her face was small, the mask concealed nearly all of her face, which made her look even more mysterious than most. Only her eyes glittered between the slits. She amused herself by languidly tilting her head, then raising one arched eyebrow above the mask. Below it, she curved her lips into a provoking smile that looked both dangerous and seductive. At least she imagined it did. Fresh laughter at herself bubbled up but remained trapped in her throat because a shadow in the doorway darkened the room.

In the glass, her eyes met those of Francis Wolfe, Earl of Warenton.

CHAPTER THREE

PARALYZED, WITH HER hands holding the mask at either side of her face, she couldn't look away. Everything inside her leapt with shock and excitement and something else she couldn't name. Her heart beat so fast it made her tremble.

He'll walk away. He has no reason to stay. Part of her wanted desperately to give him one, but that was impossible. She didn't want him to know who she was, from shame at her position or, perhaps, just because of her connection to the woman the world said he was going to marry. And she honestly didn't know if it would be better or worse for him to recognize her from the incident yesterday. Why would he even remember her?

The silence went on too long, but still he didn't vanish.

At last he said, "May I tie the strings for you?"

She dared not speak in case he recognized her

voice. So she shook her head. But even that was silly, for if she did not mean to wear the mask, the natural thing would be to lower it. And reveal her face. Which she didn't want to do for any number of confused reasons.

But it was too late. He strolled into the room, looming larger in the mirror. Without touching, he stood so close behind her that she could actually feel the warmth emanating from his body.

Her fingers jumped when his took the strings of the mask from them. She could do nothing but drop her hands and wait, breathless, while he tied the mask at the back of her head.

"A large mask for a small lady," he observed.

She drew in her breath. In her best imitation of the Renleighs' accents, she said, "It isn't mine."

A fleeting smile crossed his face. He stepped back and she didn't know if she was more relieved or disappointed. But he didn't walk towards the door. He went to the decanter on the table.

"A glass of wine?" He lifted the decanter and sniffed it. "Sherry wine," he corrected himself. "Or perhaps you'd prefer champagne?"

Champagne would be the best choice, she knew, for

then he would have to leave to fetch it and she could slip away. Only, her tongue and her feet both seemed to be frozen. By the time she turned fully to face him, he had already poured two glasses of sherry and was holding one out to her.

She licked her dry lips. Disconcertingly, his eyes dropped to follow the movement.

She shook her head. "I cannot. It would not be…appropriate."

His eyebrows lifted. "But you are not a servant."

"No," she allowed. Not strictly speaking. "But I have duties I have already avoided too long by hiding in here."

His lips tugged into a rueful smile. "I, too."

Intrigued, she took a step closer without meaning to. "You? Are you part of the British embassy?"

"Lord, no. I only came to Vienna to meet my sister and avoid going home."

Recklessly, she closed her fingers around the crystal glass and took it from him. "Why?"

He shrugged. "My brother died. I suppose I didn't want to step into his shoes and take on his responsibilities."

"But those are hardly the duties you are avoiding in

this room."

He lifted his glass in a silent toast to her and drank. "You'd be surprised."

What did he mean by that? As the Renleighs all suspected, did he mean to propose to Sylvia tonight? At least informally. He probably knew it was expected of him. Could that be the duty he spoke of? Was it really possible he did not care for the idea of marrying Sylvia?

She liked that notion altogether too much. But it made no difference. Men like Warenton had to marry well, for position, for wealth and heirs. He didn't have to like it, but he would do it.

As she sank thoughtfully onto the sofa, Lord Warenton finished his sherry and, though he wrinkled his nose, he poured himself another.

"I hear you are going to marry Miss Sylvia Renleigh," she said boldly.

He lifted the glass to his lips. "I hear that, too."

"Isn't it true?"

He regarded her thoughtfully. "What would you do with your life, Mademoiselle? If you could choose?"

Mademoiselle. So much for pretending to be English.

She smiled. "I'd run away on a pirate ship," she said lightly.

He wrinkled his nose. "Worse tyranny than any you've known here."

"But I would be the captain. The tyranny would be mine."

"That would be better," he allowed. "May I come with you as your first lieutenant?"

"If you bring the treasure map."

"Of course." He patted an imaginary pocket in his coat. "I have it with me."

"You're silly," she observed.

"No, I'm drunk," he confessed. "What's your excuse?"

"Boredom."

He nodded, thoughtfully, as though he perfectly understood. A smile began to form and hover on his lips, catching Elise's breath. He had a very persuasive, beguiling smile.

In the ballroom, the hired orchestra had struck up the next waltz. Deliberately, Warenton set down his glass and held out his hand to her. "Dance with me."

Heat thrilled through her. Temptation, hope. And understanding—he was drunk and she was his protest against doing the expected.

"I can't," she said flatly. "I would lose my position."

He blinked. "How the devil do you expect to run a pirate ship if you don't give up your current position?"

In spite of herself, laughter bubbled up.

Hearing it, he smiled back and actually took her hand, which jumped in his and then lay still. Although she knew she should withdraw it, she couldn't resist leaving it there just one moment longer.

"Come," he said. "You're masked. I can easily explain I gave you no chance to refuse with civility."

She rose to her feet. "I am quite happy to refuse *without* civility."

"But you won't," he said confidently.

It was true, part of her wanted very badly to dance with him. But the sane, sensible part which she needed to survive said candidly, "You must be more foxed than you look or you would know I don't fit whatever purpose you have. I'm wearing a mended gown and someone else's mask and—"

He tugged her to her feet. "Do you never stop talking?"

Her hand was in the crook of his arm and they were out of the door before she remembered to close her mouth. God knew how many people saw them emerge together from the antechamber. Almost worse, surely he would perceive her lameness, despite her best efforts not to favor her injured ankle.

"Who is being uncivil now?" she demanded.

"We thumb our noses at convention." He swung her into his arms and onto the dance floor. "This, my sweet, is your pirate ship."

She couldn't help her breath of laughter—despite the impropriety of his address. "Do you think they hold balls on such vessels?"

"I'm convinced pirates dance," he said firmly, waltzing her backwards and turning her.

She followed blindly, more aware of his closeness and the strength of his arm than of the dance steps. She frowned suddenly. "Yes, but were you so convinced that *I* could dance? You could have embarrassed us both horribly."

He shrugged. "I gambled on your being a quick learner, if you weren't already accomplished in the waltz. Which you are. How *did* you learn?"

"By observation." She hesitated and then confessed. "And by practicing in my bedchamber with a bolster, to a musical box my father gave me."

His lips twitched. His eyes crinkled at the corners most disarmingly when he was amused.

She said breathlessly. "This is not very like dancing with a bolster."

"I hope I compare favorably."

In truth, waltzing with him compared favorably with just about everything.

"The bolster was less bossy," she observed.

"It's called leading," he said with mock severity. "It's expected of me."

"Very well, but I am still captain."

"In everything else," he allowed. A smile flickered and vanished. "Mostly."

"I can see you will be a rebellious dog."

"On the contrary, I am loyal to a fault."

"Hmm."

She couldn't say more for he spun her around several other couples, one after another, until she felt dizzy. His arm tightened. "How is your ankle?"

In truth, she'd barely noticed it since he'd swept her onto the dance floor. But his words still deprived her of breath all over again. "You *did* recognize me!"

"Of course I did."

She frowned behind her large mask. "How?"

"I heard you laugh as I passed the antechamber door. It sounded like you so I looked in. Your height was the same and I recognized your beguiling scent at once."

"I don't wear perfume," she said dryly.

He smiled into her eyes. "You don't need to."

She couldn't breathe. She had to drag her eyes free of his before she could even think. "Then you knew me despite my English accent." She realized she'd lost it anyway at some point between the antechamber and this moment.

He laughed. "Because of it."

"Wretch," she said with what dignity she could muster.

"You're not remotely afraid of me," he observed. "Why hide?"

For the first time, she missed a step, which he disguised by immediately turning her.

"Sir, we are not equals," she said desperately. "Yesterday was not the first time we had met. I should not be dancing with you."

"There is only one reason that could possibly be true."

She stared at him, the misery of real life beginning

to rein in her ridiculous euphoria. "What is that?"

"That you do not want to."

"I don't," she whispered.

He bent his head nearer hers. "Liar."

"The music is coming to an end," she said with mingled despair and relief. "Let me go."

"Do you wish it?"

"There is no alternative."

"Give me five more minutes," he urged.

"I can't," she said in sudden anguish. "Not here…" Not in public where the world would laugh at her foolishness and the Renleighs would accuse her of God knew what. She was no real threat to Sylvia's marriage and yet…

And yet, as the waltz came to its final close, she was tugged swiftly across the floor. Other people seemed to fly past her vision. The door to the servants' staircase swung open and then closed out the ballroom behind her.

And suddenly both his arms were around her, holding her against his hard person.

By the dim candlelight on the servants' stairs, she gazed up into his shadowed face, still harsh and handsome. He was all, everything and more, that she'd ever wanted or ever could want. Life just wasn't fair.

"I am Miss Renleigh's companion," she blurted.

"I know."

Her mouth fell open. "You...*know*?"

"I remember now. Forgive me for not seeing you before."

"For you, I am not *worthy* of sight!" she exclaimed. "Don't be cruel, don't play with me! I can't—"

The rest of her words were cut off as he tore aside her mask. His mouth seized hers in the kind of kiss she'd never imagined. Deep, invasive, wonderful… Her bruised lips opened wide for him, surrendering utterly until his mouth gentled and he coaxed her with tender lips and tongue, to kiss him back.

Her heart thundered. Her stomach was in turmoil as everything in her seemed to plunge and flame. Her fingers clung to the short, soft hair at the back of his head. Her other hand, trapped between their bodies, clutched the braid of his coat. And when his hold loosened to let her breathe, she flung that arm around his neck, too, and with a sound very much like a sob, she took back his mouth.

His kisses grew slower, yet hotter and heavier, his eyes clouded in a way that excited her beyond reason.

His hand even trembled slightly as he cupped her cheek and very gradually, very gently, detached his mouth from hers.

"Tomorrow," he said huskily. "Tomorrow, I will come to you. Whatever happens, whatever you want, you will never lose from this."

She barely understood him, so lost was she in beautiful, overwhelming sensation. She could only stare up at him until he kissed her again and then again. A servant with a tray of bottles clattered down the stairs above them and brushed past them. He backed her against the wall, hiding her with his body. She'd no idea who the servant was, although the sight of her locked in the earl's arms didn't slow his footsteps in the slightest. As he swung open the door to the ballroom, a blast of music and noise shocked Elise back to reality.

She dragged her mouth free. "What are we doing?" she asked desolately. "This is *wrong*!"

"No," he said. "No. Trust me." But he did release her. He bent and picked up the fallen black mask. In the dim light, suddenly he looked like a stranger. He *was* a stranger. "May I keep this?"

She swallowed. "It was never mine."

He pocketed it. "Can you get back to the ballroom

from the top of these stairs?"

She nodded.

"Then do so. I'm sure I'm drunk enough to have believably lost my way. Until tomorrow, Elise de Sancerre." Unexpectedly, he swooped again, leaving a quick, hard kiss upon her lips, and then he vanished through the door into the ballroom.

Elise stared after him for several seconds. So he had discovered her name, too. Then she remembered that she had told him her name when he tended to her ankle. Without meaning to, she touched her lips as she turned and slowly climbed the stairs, past the kitchen along the passage to the public hallway. Here, she found the ladies' cloakroom fortunately empty and was able to re-pin her ruffled and unruly black hair back into its severe style. For a moment, she stared at her reddened lips and felt wicked. She waited for the hectic flush in her cheeks to fade. The Renleighs would know. Her eyes were sparkling with happiness.

And even that was foolish. So, for some reason, the English Wolfe liked her. By his own admission he was foxed and just as likely to have forgotten her by morning. Or even by now. What had he said? *Whatever happens, whatever you want, you will never lose from this.* From what? From her scandalous behavior?

Was he…was he about to offer her a *carte blanche*? A position as his mistress to replace the one as companion she would undoubtedly lose if and when the Renleighs got wind of her dancing with him. If she hadn't already lost it by her long absence.

She should go back. She turned away from the mirror, her heart still beating with excitement.

Whatever you want, you will never lose from this. She leaned her forehead against the door and closed her eyes with growing anguish. When he danced with her, when he kissed her, she would have gone anywhere with him in any capacity he wanted her, with or without the sanctity of marriage. But his words, his words, surely turned this spontaneous moment into some kind of transaction. Buying her as he would buy his bride, only without the honor.

It wasn't just pride that revolted against this. It was feeling. He'd only known her a little over a day—what did she expect? The fact that she'd sat in obscurity, secretly watching and listening to him, unnoticed until he'd become her obsession, did not change the fact that she was a stranger to him in every way. Surely, that mattered.

She descended the curving stairs to the ballroom, her eyes darting to discover Miss Renleigh. And the earl. The former was easily found, seated in close conversation with Lady Castlereagh, General Lisle and another lady whose name she'd forgotten. Elise sat quietly against the wall behind them and waited to be noticed.

The next dance struck up and Elise finally saw the earl leading Sylvia onto the floor. Although the girl looked as regal and impassive as ever, Elise could have sworn she was smug. She couldn't begin to describe her own feelings. But there was definitely misery in there. She'd just exchanged the old, bored, drudging misery for one far more turbulent and painful.

Miss Renleigh snapped her fingers. Elise got up at once and went to her.

"Where in the world have you been?" the old lady demanded.

"I'm sorry, Miss Renleigh. It took me some time to deliver your message and then I had to visit the cloakroom."

"Do so on your own time in the future. Fetch a glass of lemonade for Lady Castlereagh, and wine for the General and me."

"Of course," Elise murmured. There was a tray set out on a table close by and it didn't take her long to comply. She found herself wishing for other tasks just so that her eyes didn't stray to the dance floor.

It was the last dance before the unmasking and supper. The night stretched out interminably.

CHAPTER FOUR

I N ALL HIS thirty-eight years, Lord Warenton could
not remember ever being quite so obsessed with a
woman as he was with this French girl. He'd had many
love affairs in the past, some of several years standing.
But, in truth, no woman had ever played a large part in
his life. The army had been the mainstay of his
existence, women mere recreation, however exquisite.
But somehow, Elise de Sancerre had burrowed under
his skin and he was at a loss to account for it.

She was pretty, certainly, he allowed as he danced
dutifully with Sylvia Renleigh. Not the cold loveliness
of many established beauties, including the one
currently in his arms, but one less perfect and yet much
deeper. He liked, he *needed*, to look at Elise, at the
quick laughter which lit up her whole face and the
many, changing expressions in her fascinating, dark
eyes. How could he never have seen her before? How
could he have committed that crassest of sins and

regarded a human being as just part of the furniture? And not just any human being, the one he was now so desperate to make love him.

In the regiment he now commanded, he'd never looked upon any of his men as unimportant. The lowliest soldier always had his part to play and he'd always recognized and acknowledged that. Perhaps unconsciously, he still regarded civilians as of lesser importance, less worthy of the same consideration. Or perhaps, he'd just been too focused on Sylvia and whether or not he could bring himself to take Caroline's advice and marry the girl. Even now, as he made trivial conversation with her—Sylvia had no sense of humor—he could imagine her as mistress of his London house, and Warenton Park and even Questing. He could see her hosting political dinners and lavish parties and performing excellently all her duties as countess.

Where he could never imagine her was in his bed. It would be like making love to a block of ice or some inert statue...or Elise's bolster.

His breath caught in sudden laughter and Sylvia's gaze fixed on him in expectation...of what? An offer of marriage, no doubt. Thank God it had gone no further than the vague hopes of their respective families, because Warenton had no intention of marrying Sylvia now. He wanted the girl who daydreamed herself into accidents and longed to run away from the drudgery of her position to be a free pirate on the high seas.

The girl who felt so right and so damnably sweet in his arms, yielding and passionate and *joyful*. And whatever her circumstances, she was a lady in any way that mattered. Whatever her birth—and he doubted it was lowly, although he didn't greatly care if he was wrong—she would not disgrace his family. She might baffle them or cause minor outrages by her lovable eccentricities, but that only made her all the more interesting to him.

However, he wasn't stupid. She had told him she was six and twenty years old, still young compared to him, and sheltered. He'd given her a little fun tonight and assaulted her senses because he couldn't help himself. But neither could he pretend to be a young girl's romantic dream. He might have been an earl thanks to George's carelessness, but he was no Prince Charming. He wasn't far off forty years old and his personal life had been ramshackle to say the least. He'd fought too long and too hard in the thick of a seemingly endless war to be anything other than a selfish, crusty, old soldier unused to the refinements of life. That Elise's life contained few refinements at the moment he was well aware, and she deserved better.

At least he could give her wealth and position. But he had the feeling she wouldn't accept them if she didn't love him. And it was her love he wanted, that he *yearned* for. He couldn't buy that with his earldom. No one knew better than he that a few kisses didn't equate with love. He needed to court her, win her if he could…

And yet, how the devil could he do that while she was in genteel slavery to the Renleighs?

The music came to a close and he bowed to Sylvia, offering his arm so that he could return her to her aunt. As they approached, he caught sight of Elise delivering glasses to Miss Renleigh and her current companions. His heart turned over just at the sight of her, the thought of being near her.

Why, after all these years of much more simple pleasures, should this happen to him now? Love, he realized with mingled horror and awe. *I love this girl.*

Who still had to survive until tomorrow. And so, he delivered a disappointed Sylvia to her aunt, presented her with a glass of lemonade and left them with a bow. Elise again sat behind them, against the wall, looking at her hands. He couldn't guess her thoughts and wouldn't embarrass her by staring. He let his gaze glance off her and strolled away.

He left shortly afterwards, abandoning Caroline and Vernon and deciding to walk home. However, as he left the house, he saw the distinctive figure of the Prince de Talleyrand ahead of him, about to ascend to his carriage. To his surprise, de Talleyrand paused and stepped back when he noticed him.

"My lord," the French delegate greeted him. "Perhaps I may take you somewhere?"

Warenton considered. "I'd be grateful to go as far as the Kauntiz Palace, if that's your destination."

"Please." De Talleyrand bowed him inside.

Hardly blind to the rare honor, Warenton sat back as the carriage lumbered into motion and regarded his enigmatic host.

De Talleyrand smiled gently. "Doesn't one hate the gossip of a small, overcrowded city?"

"Or any other gossip," Warenton said with distaste.

"So misleading," de Talleyrand agreed. "You'll appreciate I learn a lot from gossip—among all the trivial dross. Gossip, for example, assures me you are about to contract a marriage with the beautiful Miss Renleigh."

"Gossip, we've agreed, is, indeed, largely dross."

"I thought it must be when I saw you…distinguishing Elise de Sancerre with your attentions."

Warenton sat forward, frowning. "Was I so obvious?"

De Talleyrand shrugged. "One dance with a masked stranger in a darned gown. Who cares? Unless one takes an interest in Mademoiselle de Sancerre."

Warenton narrowed his eyes. "And you do?"

De Talleyrand seemed more amused than offended. "Her father was something of a friend of mine. He's dead now, and there's little enough I can do for his only child…except look out for her."

"Which you do." Warenton sat back again, smiling faintly. "Are you warning me off, Monsieur?"

"If necessary. She is, at least, safe with the Renleighs."

"I have no intention of making her *un*safe. Since I'm glad to find someone watching over her, however distantly, I'll tell you that my intentions are, in fact, strictly honorable."

De Talleyrand blinked. "Well, damn me. I never expected *that* much safety. You English still amaze me."

Warenton began to laugh.

IT SEEMED TO Elise that she'd only just lain down in her bed and closed her eyes when she was being shaken awake again by Marta, the Austrian chambermaid.

"Mademoiselle, you must come at once. Miss Renleigh is calling for you."

Bemused, Elise wearily threw off the bedclothes. "I'll get dressed…"

"No, she means now," Marta said firmly.

Elise struggled into the robe she'd had since she was fourteen years old. "What is it? Is she ill? What time is it?"

"It's nearly nine," Marta replied, without answering the other questions.

Shaking herself fully awake, Elise hurried down the two flights of stairs to Miss Renleigh's bedchamber. There, she halted in surprise, for the old lady was not the only person present. Besides her dresser, Sylvia and her maid were also there.

Miss Renleigh, fully dressed, looked grim, her eyes sparkling with fury and outrage as she rounded on Elise.

She knows, Elise thought. Someone had told her they'd seen her dancing with Lord Warenton. Worse, maybe the servant who'd seen them kissing on the stairs had recognized her after all and carried the tale to the lady of the house.

Elise braced herself for the storm, even lifted her chin to withstand it with some dignity. Her position, undoubtedly, was lost.

"Where is it?" Miss Renleigh demanded.

Elise blinked, frowning. "Where is what, Miss Renleigh?"

"The tiara!" Miss Renleigh snapped. "What did you do with it?"

Elise's knees sagged with relief. "The tiara? I brought it back from Miss Sylvia as you asked and gave it to you. You didn't like it with your costume, so you took it off and threw it on the bed."

Everyone continued to stare at her.

"And then?" Miss Renleigh said frostily.

"I went to change as you bade me. I haven't seen it

since." She glanced at Beetson, Miss Renleigh's maid. "Did you not put it away?"

Beetson sniffed superciliously, though her eyes fell. "Yes, Mamzelle, of course, but it isn't there now."

"And Miss Sylvia did not borrow it for any reason?"

"In the middle of the night?" Miss Renleigh said scathingly. "Stop blaming other people. Return it to me now and I will not involve the authorities. But either way, you will pack your bags and be gone."

Elise's jaw dropped as understanding finally struck. Her knees gave way and she sank down on the bed, only to leap up again in mingled anger and shame and pride.

"*I*? You think *I* stole your tiara? On what grounds could you possibly imagine that?"

"You are French," Sylvia said with contempt. "You are poor. And you had the opportunity."

Elise could hardly deny the first two—though how they equated with "thief" was another argument. "Opportunity?" she repeated. "When, in God's name? I am *never* alone!"

"You will calm your temper," Miss Renleigh said icily. "Go and dress and think about what you have done. Then come to the morning room in one hour. Bring the tiara—and your bags—with you."

Miss Renleigh turned her back deliberately and Sylvia followed suit. So did the maids with silent triumph. They must have imagined she usurped their positions somehow... Were they responsible for blaming Elise? Or for taking the tiara in the first place? Certainly, Beetson had lied about putting it away...

With deliberation, Beetson scooped up Miss Renleigh's laundry from the foot of the bed, stuffing it into an already bulging linen bag. No one said a word.

Never in her life had Elise felt quite so lonely and rejected. She'd worked herself ragged for these people for three years, doing everything and more ever asked of her, however unnecessary or trivial or just plain spiteful, and never once complaining. And yet they could accuse her of this, *believe* this of her.

Blindly, she turned on her heel and left.

CAROLINE STARED AT him over her morning hot chocolate which she was drinking in bed over a newspaper. "You want me to *what*?"

"Invite Mademoiselle de Sancerre here to stay with

you," Warenton repeated patiently.

"Why the devil would I do that?" Caroline demanded. "I've barely spoken to the woman! Frankly, I didn't even register her name until you told me!"

"It's an old and noble name, according to de Talleyrand. She fled the revolution as a child with her family."

"That may be," Caroline said impatiently. "But she's hardly in need of a home now. She's companion to Miss Renleigh."

"Drudge to Miss Renleigh," Warenton corrected.

"That may be, too," Caroline allowed. "Unfortunately, it tends to come with the position. But it is a respectable and genteel post. I don't understand why you want *me* to step in. I don't *need* a companion. I don't want one!"

"It isn't for you," Warenton admitted. "It's for me. I feel responsible for her."

Caroline's frown of incomprehension began to smooth, her eyes to widen with furious understanding. She lifted her cup as though she would fling it at him.

"How dare you, Francis? I will not give house room to your mistresses!"

"Why not?" he asked sardonically, closing his fingers around the threatening cup and removing it from his sister's grip. "Because Vernon wouldn't like it?"

"Yes," she said with her usual honesty.

"Well, she isn't my mistress, so Vernon needn't worry."

"No, but *I* will! I'll not have you seducing noble maidens beneath my roof either!"

"Well, at least she is a *noble maiden,* now."

Caroline narrowed her eyes.

Warenton flung up his hands. "Very well, very well, I've finished teasing you. I will move to other lodgings when she comes here, so it is all straight and above board. The truth is, I wish to court her and marry her, if she'll have me."

Caroline blinked. "*Have* you? She'll bite your hand off to be Countess of Warenton!"

"You must see," Warenton pursued, "that I cannot court her under the same roof as Sylvia Renleigh."

"You mean after you raised expectations in that quarter!" Caroline snapped.

Warenton lifted his eyebrows. "I did no such thing. You and Miss Renleigh between you may have exaggerated my interest. Judging by her expression last night, I imagine you did. But I won't be pushed into it by any of you. I told you to leave it be while I considered. Well I have considered. She and I would not suit."

Caroline swallowed. "I hate it when you talk like that."

"Like what?"

"Like Papa. As if you know you're right."

"Caro, *you* know I'm right. Sylvia may yet catch her duke or prince. I want Elise de Sancerre."

"But *why*?" Caroline demanded.

Warenton stood up. "I'm sure you'll understand when you meet her. Come with me in an hour or write the note as I asked you."

Caroline pushed back her tray. "Oh, I'm coming," she assured him. "I wouldn't miss this for the world."

CHAPTER FIVE

E LISE ENTERED THE morning room with her bag in one hand and her old cloak over her arm. Miss Renleigh wasn't present. Only Sylvia sat in the armchair by the fire, her back perfectly straight. Sylvia watched as she slowly approached and laid the bag at her feet. It contained all her worldly possessions, save what she wore on her back.

"Miss Sylvia," she said as calmly as she could. "You cannot truly believe I would steal from this family or from anyone else. You cannot think I took the tiara."

Sylvia didn't blink. "I don't care whether you did or not," she said frankly. "I want you gone."

Elise frowned helplessly. "But why? I run scores of errands for you every day. I have never done you one iota of harm."

"Liar," Sylvia uttered with sudden, quite unexpected viciousness. "Did you think I would not see you dancing with Lord Warenton? I did. I saw you coming out of the antechamber with him, too. And then you both disappeared for quite some time."

Elise could not deny it, although she felt mortified to be found out. Not because she regretted or was ashamed of what she'd done; because she didn't want it sullied by other people's interpretations.

"I talked to him. I danced with him. Once. Even if I'd danced with him all night, you know it would make no difference to you. I am no one."

"And yet," Sylvia said flatly, "he did not propose."

Some wicked, selfish part of her couldn't help being glad. If he had kissed Elise and offered marriage to Sylvia on the same night…

"Perhaps he will today or tomorrow. Please, Sylvia, if you know what happened to the tiara, tell me."

Sylvia's eyes flashed with disdain. The door opened and Miss Renleigh came in with her nephew, Lord Renleigh, who looked both harassed and uncomfortable.

"I will tell you," Sylvia said. "*You* took it. Everything points to you."

"Nothing points to me!" Elise exclaimed. "Nothing whatsoever. You just said as much when you told me you didn't care about the truth of the matter!"

"I said no such thing," Sylvia lied without so much as a flicker.

Elise took an impulsive step forward and Sylvia threw both hands up as if to ward her off. "Don't let her near me!" she cried with a shudder.

Renleigh immediately jumped between them. "Here, now, let's sort this out in a civilized manner," he pleaded. "Why don't we all sit down?"

"I'd rather stand," Elise insisted.

"You *will* stand," Miss Renleigh said grimly. "Have you brought the tiara back to me?"

"Of course I haven't. I didn't take it in the first place, as you should know perfectly well. Nothing has ever been stolen from you as long as I've been in your employ."

"Well, there were a few bottles of wine in London," Renleigh said reluctantly.

Elise stared at him. "Do you imagine I was drinking myself to sleep every night? If so, I wonder how I managed to rouse myself twice a night for Miss Renleigh and still get up at seven every morning."

"Don't take that tone with your betters," Miss Renleigh snapped. "Especially when I smelled wine on your breath last night."

She couldn't help flushing. She had, indeed, drunk a glass of sherry with Lord Warenton. "Pray take the cost of one glass of sherry from my wages, if there's anything left of them. If not, be assured I will pay you back from my next post."

"Do you plan to pay for the tiara that way, too?" Miss Renleigh sneered.

"No, for I did not take the tiara."

"So you say," Sylvia interjected. "Perhaps you could explain to us where you were between dancing with Lord Warenton and fetching drinks for my aunt and General Lisle?"

At that moment, the door opened and the butler announced, "Lady Caroline Vernon and Lord Warenton."

Even the sound of his name caused Elise's stomach to somersault. The servants must have been ordered to admit the earl whenever he called. Dismay and sudden hope warred across Sylvia's face. Miss Renleigh scowled, no doubt at the bad timing, but hastily smoothed her face to smiles as she went forward to greet her somewhat early callers.

Normally, Elise would have whisked herself away to the back of the room upon the arrival of any guests.

But this morning, pride and sheer stubbornness kept here where she was in the middle of the room, surrounded by Renleighs.

Lady Caroline walked in, smiling amiably. On her heels came Lord Warenton himself, instantly shrinking the room by his size and sheer, commanding personality. Today, he wore civilian dress, buff pantaloons with a plain black coat and a somewhat carelessly tied cravat when compared to Renleigh's highly elaborate one. But there was no mistaking the breadth of his shoulders or the strength in his thickly-muscled legs. Every inch of his fine, powerful person had been pressed against her as he'd kissed her last night…

She would not remember that here. She wouldn't. He'd come to offer for Sylvia as he'd always intended. Part of him didn't want to marry her, of course, or, probably, anyone, but the death of his brother was forcing his hand. Last night, he'd been intoxicated, perhaps rebellious, a last fling of freedom before he bowed to duty.

"Do forgive us for calling so early," Lady Caroline was saying civilly. "I hope we haven't come at a bad moment?"

"Of course not," Miss Renleigh said graciously. "Do

please sit down."

"Thank you so much for the ball last night," Lady Caroline began. "Such a wonderful evening."

Miss Renleigh inclined her head, murmuring some platitude that Elise barely heard for her panic at Lord Warenton's approach.

"Expect you want a private word with me, Warenton," Renleigh said knowingly.

Oh no, I can't hear this... From instinct, Elise was already brushing past Warenton and making for the door.

"Not really," Warenton said. She could feel his eyes on her face, but refused to look up as she walked on. This room had never seemed so spacious until she was so anxious to get out of it.

"Oh, don't run off my dear," Lady Caroline said, catching her hand as she tried to escape. "I was hoping to speak to you while I was here."

Astonished, Elise lifted her eyes to Lady Caroline's. She read intrigue, suspicion and, surely, voracious interest. "To me?" she said, believing she must, somehow, have misunderstood.

"Why yes, I was hoping Miss Renleigh might part with you, at least for a while. I wanted to ask you to stay with me for a little while."

Elise began to wonder wildly if both brother and sister were actually insane. It could have explained a great deal. She stared at Caroline in bafflement. "Why?"

Lady Caroline's breath caught, as if she were wrestling with laughter. On any other occasion, Elise might have liked her for that. Right now, she was far too agitated to appreciate anything that kept her in this room.

"Truthfully, because I recently heard something of your story and would like to know you better," Lady Caroline said, with only the faintest quaver in her voice.

Elise had no idea what to reply to that. Her first instinct was to look to Lord Warenton for guidance, but since she couldn't do that, she turned and looked back at Miss Renleigh instead.

"I should be very careful, Lady Caroline," Miss Renleigh said, "before I invited a thief into my home."

Elise closed her eyes. At least it gave her the illusion that the floor had swallowed her up. Until Lord Warenton spoke coldly into the silence.

"I believe my sister invited Mademoiselle de Sancerre."

"They are one and the same," Miss Renleigh said tartly. "This ingrate has stolen the diamond and ruby tiara that has been in our family for nigh on two hundred years. I have given her the chance to return it without prosecution, but since she has failed to do that, I have no choice but to involve the authorities. I would spare you the embarrassment, Lady Caroline."

"You make a serious allegation," Warenton said evenly. "What proof do you imagine you have?"

Imagine. What proof do you imagine *you have?* Elise opened her eyes, gazing at Lord Warenton in wonder. He didn't believe it. He knew she hadn't done this.

Renleigh said cheerfully, "Good question. Mademoiselle was just about to tell us where she was yesterday evening when everyone agrees she disappeared from the ball."

"Renleigh," Sylvia said sharply. "Not now."

"Well you brought it up," Renleigh retorted. "Seems to me it all hinges on that."

"Does it," Warenton said. It wasn't really a question and it was spoken with a sardonic contempt she had never heard him use before. "What time did this so-called disappearance occur?"

"Just after she danced with you, apparently, before the unmasking," Renleigh said.

It struck Elise that Renleigh didn't actually believe she was a thief either. None of them did and yet all the Renleighs would prosecute her for it. Because she'd danced with the man Sylvia wished to marry.

"Then the matter is easily solved," Warenton said, flicking a speck of dust from the cuff of his coat. "Mademoiselle de Sancerre was with me."

"Renleigh, you imbecile," Sylvia uttered between her teeth.

This, of course, was exactly the admission Sylvia didn't want made in company. She didn't want Warenton backed into a corner where he had to save Elise's honor or lose his own. Now he had been forced to save Elise from accusations of theft by compromising her. She would never obtain another respectable position and so he was obliged to marry her.

Elise drew in a shuddering breath. "I was not with Lord Warenton," she announced.

Lady Caroline's eyes widened. She couldn't look at Warenton, though he said "Elise!" in a frustrated kind of way.

"There you are!" Miss Renleigh crowed. "By your own admission! You stole my tiara!"

"She admitted no such thing," Warenton said irritably. "Mademoiselle, you must tell the truth and be done with this. You *know* you were with me."

"I was not," Elise said clearly.

Miss Renleigh turned to her nephew. "Renleigh, send to General Lisle. His prospective son-in-law is something to do with the Austrian police."

"That would be ridiculous," Warenton said calmly. "Miss Renleigh, to establish the truth of this, you will allow me five minutes' private speech with Mademoiselle de Sancerre."

Miss Renleigh tilted her head stubbornly. "I will not."

It was a mistake. Even Elise could see that he would never now ally himself with her family. Warenton held the old lady's gaze until she lowered it.

"Then," he observed, "there is no more to be said. Mademoiselle, please accompany my sister to the waiting carriage. She will send for your things. Miss Renleigh is apparently determined to be made a laughing stock. Good day, ma'am. Miss Sylvia. Renleigh."

VIENNA WOLFE

Somehow, Elise found herself in the cold, fresh air. Someone, surely Warenton, took her cloak and placed it around her shoulders. Lady Caroline held her arm and urged her into the waiting carriage. She only woke from her daze when Warenton climbed in, too, and sat opposite them.

"Wait," she said in sudden panic. "I can't go with you. I won't. I won't be made to marry you."

"No one will make you do anything," Warenton said.

"But I think what she means," Lady Caroline said shrewdly as the horses pulled away, "is that she won't have *you* made to marry *her*. You're quite right, Francis. She is something out of the ordinary." She patted Elise's hand. "You needn't worry, you know. The Renleighs will never repeat that story, since it reflects badly on Sylvia's charms and frustrated hopes. I very much doubt you'll hear anything more about the theft either. If you ask me, Renleigh himself took the damned tiara to pay his debts."

"That was my first thought," Warenton admitted.

"And mine," Elise confessed. "But his manner was all wrong. I don't think he did take it. I don't think the maids did either, though they'll be glad enough to be

73

rid of me."

"Sylvia?" Warenton suggested.

"The same." Elise frowned. Then, abruptly, she laughed. "I know exactly where the wretched thing is. Please, stop the carriage and I'll fetch it for them."

"Oh no," Warenton said. "You shan't set foot in that house again."

Elise scowled at him. "I want them to eat their nasty words in my presence."

"They're more likely to turn it against you and say you put it wherever it is you find it. Write them a note."

Elise considered. "Very well." She looked up and met Warenton's half-frustrated, half-amused gaze and, in spite of everything, she wanted to laugh.

"Put us out of our misery," he suggested. "Where is it?"

"With her laundry. It's happened before. Miss Renleigh throws everything on the bed and Beetson, her maid, bundles it all into a bag. Every so often, reticules, earrings, even necklaces end up there. Usually, she doesn't notice until someone returns them to her."

"Then why is she blaming you for the tiara?" Caroline demanded. She seemed rather flatteringly outraged on Elise's behalf.

Elise shrugged. "Because Sylvia suggested it to her. And the maids went along with it. I knew Beetson was lying when she said she'd put the tiara away. I was just too tired and too much taken by surprise to see what really happened. Until now."

Warenton sat back in his seat. "Damned if I'm not disappointed," he drawled. "I was hoping this was your first act of piracy."

And although she didn't mean to, Elise met his gaze and smiled.

>>>><<<<

"THANK YOU FOR all of this," Elise said to Lady Caroline, somewhat shyly. She and her rather pathetically few belongings had been installed in the apartment's spare bedchamber. She had written a note to Miss Renleigh saying merely that Beetson should look in the linen bag where previously two reticules, three earrings and a necklace had been found in the last three years. Lady Caroline's Austrian footman had taken the letter and returned with Elise's bag.

"I expect they looked through it first," Caroline said contemptuously, "and were disappointed not to find the tiara."

"And all the wine they claim I stole in London. Unless I drank it all."

Caroline laughed and sat down on the bed. "Unpleasant people. I really had no idea!"

Elise said on a rush, "You must let me know how I can assist you while I'm here. If only you'll give me a reference, I'm sure I can obtain another position quite quickly and be out of your way."

Caroline waved that aside. "Of course, if it's what you want."

"It is. Thank you."

Caroline eyed her somewhat curiously. "He wasn't there to offer for Sylvia, you know. Any expectation of that event was largely conjured by me and Miss Renleigh. I suppose I am anxious to see him settled and happy. And I had heard only good things about Sylvia."

Elise nodded. She didn't know what else she could say or do.

"My brother," Caroline said carefully, "is never pushed into anything. By anyone. For what it's worth, I have never seen him so taken with a female."

Elise lifted her gaze to Caroline's. "Don't. Please

don't."

"You don't like him?" Caroline seemed surprised. In any case, it was so far from the truth that it drew a strange choking sound from Elise—half-sob and half-laughter.

"How could I not like him?"

Caroline smiled and stood. "Then come into the drawing room and be comfortable. My husband will be home soon and will very much like to meet you."

It already seemed odd to have nothing to do but be in the company of someone who expected nothing from her and, moreover, seemed glad of her being there.

She sat on the sofa in the comfortable drawing room and tried to make herself think of the best way to acquire a new position. After some idle chat, Lady Caroline wandered away, so Elise, curiously relaxed, picked up the newspaper from the table and spread it on the sofa to look for advertised positions. She'd just found the right section, when Lord Warenton strolled in.

She jumped to her feet in sudden, foolish panic and he paused, bowing slightly without releasing her gaze.

"My presence disturbs you," he observed.

"Yes," she admitted, before realizing how rude that sounded. "I mean, no, of course not."

He raised his brows, a faint smile forming on his lips.

"Oh dear," she said ruefully, "I sound so confused. I *am* confused!"

"By me?"

An unhappy smile tugged at her lips. "By me, mainly." But that wasn't strictly true, so she added reluctantly, "And by you."

He regarded her for several moments, while her heartbeat drummed in her breast, quickening her breath. He seemed so large and distant and unreachable, quite unlike the man who'd danced with her last night. And yet he still affected her this way. She still yearned for him, as she always had, even before he'd looked at her.

He stirred. "Circumstances have made this more difficult than I intended."

She swallowed, tearing her gaze free at last. It was the only way to deal with the pain of her vanishing dreams. "Please," she managed in a rather choked voice. "I know you have done this from kindness. I expect nothing from you. I *want* nothing from you."

His gaze burned into her averted face. He advanced towards her until, in fresh panic, she tried to turn away. But his hand shot out, taking hold of her chin and tipping it upward, forcing her to look at him once more.

"Nothing?" he repeated. "That would disappoint me."

She grasped his wrist, trying in vain to loosen his grip on her chin. "I mean, I do not, I *will* not, hold you to anything that happened last night. You'd had too much wine and I should have known better—"

"Better than what?" he interrupted. "Better than to dance with me? To kiss me?"

Her face flamed.

He said, "If you regret it, if you wish me gone from your life, you have only to say the word. I've found lodgings with a friend until I return to England. Caroline will still stand your friend. As I said last night, you will lose nothing."

Her eyes widened. "That is what you meant! I thought—" She broke off, flushing even more.

"You thought what?" he asked softly.

"That you meant to offer me a *carte blanche*," she said in a rush.

His fingers tightened for an instant on her chin, then relaxed, moving in a gentle caress that made her skin tingle. He looked neither offended nor found out. "And if I did, you would throw it back in my face."

"I don't know," she blurted, and at least had the satisfaction of seeing she'd surprised him. His eyes widened imperceptibly. "If you loved me, if I loved you, I would go anywhere with you."

His breath caught. His fingers moved from her chin, cupping her cheek with something very like wonder.

"So you see," she continued, her voice quite steady, "whatever your feelings, there is no need to offer me marriage. I would *hate* to be married for such a stupid reason as supposed comp—"

The rest of her words were lost in his mouth as it swooped and devoured her own. With a sob, she flung her arm around his neck, kissing him back with blind, instinctive passion.

After a few moments, she tried to pull away. "You can't love me," she whispered against his lips. "Not in a day."

"A day, an hour, a minute, it makes no difference. And I *swear* I will make you love me, too…"

She took his face between her hands. "Oh, you idiot!" she said shakily. "I loved you before you even knew I existed."

He stared at her, hope and wonder warring across his normally calm face.

"Idiot is right," he said, his thumb rubbing the corner of her lips before he bent his head, once more, and kissed her with such tenderness she wanted to weep. There was no one in the world but him.

Until Lady Caroline's voice interrupted. "There. I told you they would be married. Elise, my husband. Vernon, Mademoiselle de Sancerre. Shall we leave them for five minutes?"

Warenton's lips loosened, smiling against Elise's before he raised his head. "No, don't run off. You may be the first to congratulate us. Elise has just agreed to be my wife."

CHAPTER SIX

A MONTH LATER, on Christmas Eve, they were married in the village church at Warenton, watched by hordes of the Wolfe family, heavily braided army officers and as many local people as could squash into the church and grounds. As they emerged onto the church porch, in the cold winter sunshine, they were cheered and waved and then ushered into their waiting carriage. Elise clasped the earl's hand tightly throughout the short drive to Warenton House, a beautiful mansion built early in the last century.

The night's frost lingered in the bright cold of the day, making everything sparkle. It was a beautiful day to be married. Even nature seemed to be celebrating with them.

On her husband's arm, Elise stepped over the threshold of her new domain. Only the two nights she'd already spent here with Lady Caroline and a pack of other Wolfes, prevented the surroundings from overwhelming her. Wolfe ancestors stretching back for centuries, gazed down upon her as she walked across the massive entrance hall and climbed the grand staircase, both lined with liveried servants and smartly turned-out maids. She would get to know them all in time.

It was a massive undertaking, a great adventure, and she was looking forward to all of it. But right now, all she could really think about was the powerful man at her side.

"Where are we going?" she murmured as they passed the first landing. On this floor, the huge, formal dining room had been made ready for the wedding breakfast, as had the drawing room where they would greet their guests.

"Guess," he said, leading her up the next flight. There were no servants here.

Her heart thundering, she couldn't speak. She had already seen her private apartments—a luxurious, feminine bedchamber and a cozy sitting room. It was the sitting room he took her to, first, and when he turned in the opposite direction to the bedchamber door, she didn't know whether to be relieved or furiously disappointed.

"Our guests will be here any moment," she managed.

"They may wait for just a little while." He pushed the wall and a door she hadn't even seen, disguised as it was to appear part of the wall, opened into a much more masculine domain.

This was his. Leather chairs, a mahogany desk, books, odd objects from his days fighting in India, Portugal, Spain and France. She gazed about her in wonder as they crossed the room to anther door, already open to show the chamber beyond.

She swallowed hard and let him lead her there, too. A huge, curtained bed dominated the room. She couldn't take her eyes off it.

He said, "I believe it is customary in civilized marriages for a husband to visit his wife when he wishes to exert his conjugal rights. Neither of us are slaves to convention, so I want to be sure you understand something."

With strange reluctance, she dragged her gaze from the bed and, almost fearfully, up to his face.

"Between us, there are no rights," he said gravely. "Only desires and wishes. I will want you all the time, but you are always at liberty to send me packing. I'll think no less of you. It is my desire to sleep every night with you in my arms, whether that is here in this room, in your bedchamber, or on the floor of some barn. Again, you may choose when that happens, where it happens, or even if it happens."

A strange wonder began to fill her. She'd married a harsh, powerful, virile man who was strong enough to let her choose rather than exert his undoubted authority under every law and custom.

He raised her hand to his lips and softly kissed it. "I brought you here to show you that my chamber is yours whenever you wish it."

In spite of her nervousness, she couldn't help her quick smile. "Is that really why you brought me here?" she teased.

An answering sparkle lit up his eyes. "In part. I also want to make a suggestion."

"What?" she asked breathlessly.

"I would like," he murmured, "to make love to you now, before we greet our guests. I would like to give you pleasure and take my own, and make it so sweet, so intense and so satisfying that you long for me again, all through the party. I don't want you to fear your wedding night. I want you to crave it."

Her whole body tingled at his words. Strange heat curled through her belly. "What must I do?"

"Whatever you like. We could begin with a kiss."

"I would like that," she whispered, parting her lips as he bent his head.

His kiss began softly, tenderly, causing butterflies to dance and plunge deep within her. At the touch of his tongue, curling heat burst into flames and she opened wide to him, gasping, throwing both arms around him to draw him closer.

He groaned with clear delight. Rather than fearing the movement of his fingers unlacing her gown, she wriggled with pleasure at their touch. Gown, under-gown and chemise soon lay in a puddle around her feet and she stood before him totally naked.

His eyes drank her in, devoured her. Her breathing came in pants. God help her, she didn't feel remotely ashamed. Instead, she felt at once gloriously powerful and deliciously weak. With a muttered curse, he swept her up against him, his buttons abrading the sensitive skin of her breasts, and carried her the few paces to the bed.

"I want to see *you*," she whispered, among the pillows as he lay over her.

"You shall," he assured her, shrugging out of his coat. He drew her hands inside his shirt before he lowered his head to her throat, dragging his mouth downwards to her breasts. She thought she would die of bliss.

Afterwards, when she dwelled on this first coupling, she could never quite be sure of the order things happened. She was sure he was at least partly inside her before all his clothes were off. It never seemed to matter. His hot, smooth back undulated beneath her hands in the intense, sweet motion of love, showing her, teaching her, bringing her by slow, patient, oh-so-delicious stages to a blinding joy she had never expected.

Afterwards, she lay in his arms, her hair falling across his still heaving chest as she lazily kissed it. She smiled. She felt, as the English said, like the cat with the cream.

"And now," he said, "we can join our guests. You may enjoy the party without worrying about what's to come."

"We can," she agreed. Her smile broadening, she rolled herself boldly over his body, and kissed his mouth.

"Or," she murmured against his lips, "perhaps we could do this just once more before we go down."

"It would hurt you," he said, closing his arms around her and tumbling her again beneath him. "And even I am not so selfish."

Her disappointment must have stood out clearly on her face, for a rather wolfish smile spread over his. "On the other hand…" He kissed her, open-mouthed, with blatant sensuality. "On the other hand, there are many routes to pleasure. Let me show you another…"

⋙⋘

AND SO IT was some time before the newlyweds joined their guests for the wedding breakfast. Opinions varied as to whether the earl had been swiftly exerting his conjugal rights—after all, an heir was needed and, by tradition, the groom should be inebriated by tonight—or if his bride had thrown some kind of tantrum. Whatever, they appeared to be in perfect accord as they sat side by side beneath the portraits of more long-dead Wolfes.

"Who is that?" Elise asked him once, indicating a modern painting of an armored knight on horseback, his helmet held in front of him as he gazed fearlessly into the distance from just one eye. The other was covered by a square of black cloth.

"Our progenitor," the earl said. "The semi-legendary Sir William de Wolfe, the first earl. A fierce, thirteenth century warlord who let nothing stand in his way, by all accounts. My father commissioned it, insisting it be painted from actual descriptions of him in surviving texts."

"I always said he sounded like Francis," Caroline contributed from his other side. "I'm sure that's why Papa had it done."

Elise regarded the picture thoughtfully. "Do you think he'd be pleased that you married an enemy?"

"France is no longer our enemy," Warenton pointed out. He glanced up at his ancestor and smiled. "But yes, I think he would. I think he'd understand perfectly."

Mary Lancaster's Newsletter

If you enjoyed *Vienna Wolfe* and would like to keep up with Mary's new releases and other book news, please sign up to Mary's mailing list to receive her occasional Newsletter – and a free sampler of her other books!

OTHER BOOKS BY MARY LANCASTER

VIENNA WALTZ (The Imperial Season, Book 1)

VIENNA WOODS (The Imperial Season, Book 2)

VIENNA DAWN (The Imperial Season, Book 3)

REBEL OF ROSS

A PRINCE TO BE FEARED: the love story of Vlad
Dracula

AN ENDLESS EXILE

A WORLD TO WIN

About Mary Lancaster

Mary Lancaster's first love was historical fiction. Her other passions include coffee, chocolate, red wine and black and white films – simultaneously where possible. She hates housework.

As a direct consequence of the first love, she studied history at St. Andrews University. She now writes full time at her seaside home in Scotland, which she shares with her husband, three children and a small, crazy dog.

Connect with Mary on-line:

Email Mary:
Mary@MaryLancaster.com

Website:
www.MaryLancaster.com

Newsletter sign-up:
http://eepurl.com/b4Xoif

Facebook Author Page:
facebook.com/MaryLancasterNovelist

Facebook Timeline:
facebook.com/mary.lancaster.1656

Twitter:
twitter.com/MaryLancNovels